Easy to Read! • Easy to Draw!

Dinosaurs

Library of Congress Cataloging-in-Publication Data Available

ISBN: 0-8431-0435-X   A B C D E F G H I J

Dinosaurs

By Joan Holub

Illustrated by
Joan Holub and Dana Regan

PSS!
PRICE STERN SLOAN

Dinosaurs lived long ago.
I'm sad they're all gone now.
But I can draw them anytime,
and I will show you how.

Angry **Allosaurus**
had sharp teeth in its jaws.
Its front feet were like weapons.
Each one had three big claws.

(Say it like this: al-oh-SAW-rus.)

Use these shapes to draw an Allosaurus.

Here's **Ankylosaurus**.
It had armor and could fight.
It swung its tail at enemies
with all its dino might.

(Say it like this: AN-kee-loh-SAW-rus.)

Use these shapes to draw an Ankylosaurus.

Big **Brachiosaurus**
ate leaves and did not hunt.
In the back, it had short legs
and longer ones in front.

(Say it like this: BRAK-ee-oh-SAW-rus.)

Use these shapes to draw a Brachiosaurus.

Small **Coelophysis**
liked eating bugs for lunch.
Lizards were a tasty treat.
It ate them by the bunch.

(Say it like this: SEEL-oh-FI-sis.)

Use these shapes to draw a Coelophysis.

Silly **Corythosaurus**
used to honk and bellow.
It had a helmet on its head—
What a funny-looking fellow.

(Say it like this: ko-RITH-oh-SAW-rus.)

Use these shapes to draw a Corythosaurus.

At a museum in Chicago,
there's a dinosaur named Sue.

Here's scary **Deinonychus**.
Its name means "awful claw."
It ran fast to grab and gulp
small dinosaurs it saw.

(Say it like this: DIE-no-NIKE-us.)

Use these shapes to draw a Deinonychus.

Slowpoke **Diplodocus**
snacked on plants all day.
It whipped its tail back and forth
keeping enemies away.

(Say it like this:
dip-LOD-oh-kus.)

Use these shapes to draw a Diplodocus.

1

2

3

4

5

Super-fast **Iguanodon**
had special, spiky thumbs.
It used them while out hunting.
Look out! Here it comes!

(Say it like this: i-GWAH-noh-don.)

Use these shapes to draw an Iguanodon.

Mother **Maiasaura**
laid her eggs inside a mound.
Then millions of years later,
their fossil bones were found.

(Say it like this: MY-a-SAW-ruh.)

Use these shapes to draw a Maiasaura.

1

2

3

4

5

6

7

Scaly **Nodosaurus**
had tough, thick skin with bumps.
Just like an armadillo,
its armored back had lumps.

(Say it like this: NODE-oh-SAW-rus.)

Use these shapes to draw a Nodosaurus.

1

2

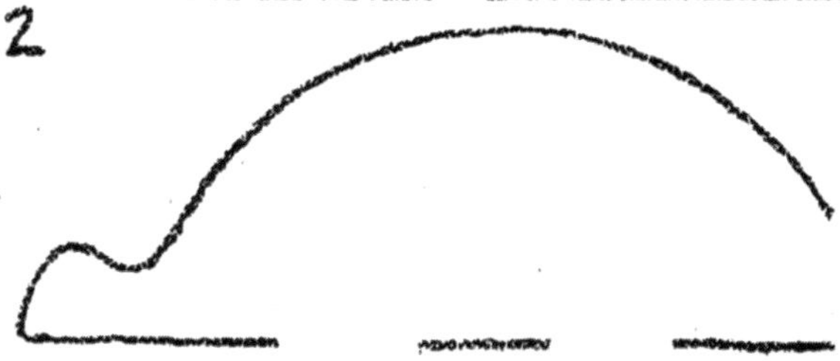

3

4

5

6

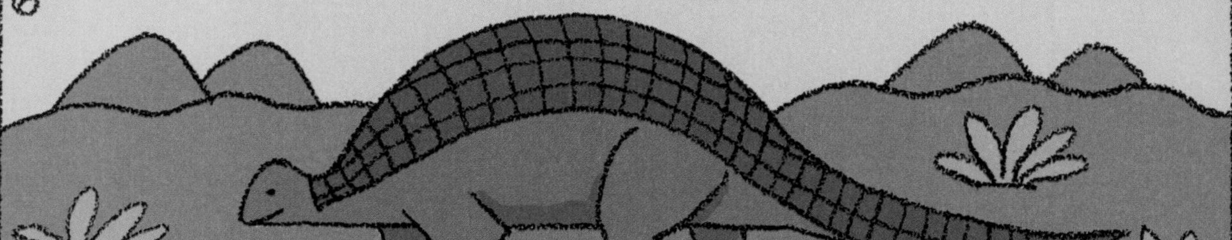

Busy **paleontologists**
study bones for clues.
They search the world for dinosaurs
with their digging crews.

Noisy **Parasaurolophus**
had the oddest nose around.
It was longer than its head
and made a foghorn sound.

(Say it like this: par-a-SAW-roh-LOAF-us.)

Use these shapes to draw a Parasaurolophus.

1

2

3

4

5

6

7

8

See the sail on **Spinosaurus**?
It kept its temperature just right.
Not too hot on sunny days,
and not too cold at night.

(Say it like this: SPINE-oh-SAW-rus.)

Use these shapes to draw a Spinosaurus.

1

2

3

4

5

6

7

Here's mighty **Stegosaurus**—
It had plates along its back.
But they could not protect it
from a dinosaur's attack.

(Say it like this: STEG-oh-SAW-rus.)

Use these shapes to draw a Stegosaurus.

1

2

3

4

5

Dangerous **Triceratops**
could fight off all its foes
with two horns right above its eyes
and one horn on its nose.

(Say it like this: tri-SER-oh-tops.)

Use these shapes to draw a Triceratops.

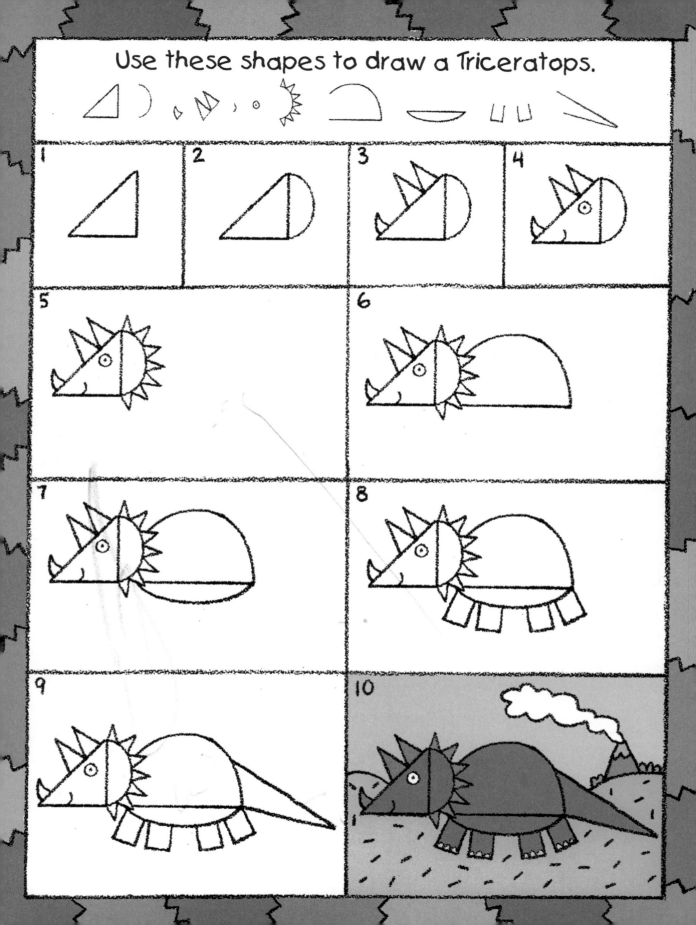

Terrible **Tyrannosaurus**
loved to fight and eat.
Can you guess its favorite food?
Yum, yum! Dino meat!

(Say it like this: tie-RAN-oh-SAW-rus.)

Use these shapes to draw a Tyrannosaurus.

1

2

3

4

5

6

7

I can draw a dinosaur
from my imagination.
There's never been one quite like this.
It's my very own creation!

Tutu-rannosaurus Rex

Parachute-aurolophus

Crown-ythosaurus

Bee-rachiosaurus

BZZZ

I can draw a dinosaur
that's happy, tired, or sad.
I can draw a dinosaur
that's scary, mean, and mad.

Now you can try!

The **Mesozoic** era,
millions of years ago,
is when these dinosaurs once lived.
Do you see some that you know?

The dinosaurs all disappeared.
And no one knows their fate.
I'll never see a real, live one.

But I still think they're great!